Big Dog and Little Dog visit the Moon

Selina Young

Blue Bananas

"⭐ for Louie and Tail
the real
Big Dog and
Little Dog ⭐"

Big Dog and Little Dog visit the Moon

Selina Young

BLue Bananas

Other titles in the bunch:

Big Dog and Little Dog Go Sailing
Big Dog and Little Dog Visit the Moon
Colin and the Curly Claw
Dexter's Journey
Follow the Swallow
"Here I Am!" said Smedley

Horrible Haircut
Magic Lemonade
The Magnificent Mummies
Midnight in Memphis
Peg
Shoot!

Crabtree Publishing Company
www.crabtreebooks.com

PMB 16A, 350 Fifth Avenue
Suite 3308
New York, NY 10118

612 Welland Avenue
St. Catharines, Ontario
Canada, L2M 5V6

Young, Selina.
  Big Dog and Little Dog visit the moon / Selina Young.
     p. cm. -- (Blue Bananas)
Summary: Because the moon looks sad, Big Dog and Little Dog
build a rocket to fly there, "lumpity, bumpity through the night," to
cheer him up
     ISBN 0-7787-0849-7-- ISBN 0-7787-0895-0 (pbk.)
     [1. Dogs--Fiction. 2. Moon--Fiction. 3. Cheerfulness--Fiction. 4.
Space flight to the moon--Fiction.] I. Title. II. Series.
PZ7.Y8792 Bk 2002
[E]--dc21
                                        2001032446
                                        LC

Published by Crabtree Publishing in 2002
First published in 1996 by Mammoth
an imprint of Egmont Children's Books Limited
Text and illustration copyright © Selina Young 1996
The Author has asserted her moral rights.
Paperback ISBN 0-7787-0895-0
Reinforced Hardcover Binding ISBN 0-7787-0849-7

One night, when Big Dog and Little Dog were going home, they saw the moon in the sky. He was big and yellow, but he looked sad. "Poor Moon," said Little Dog.

Big Dog and Little Dog went home

and made plans to build a rocket.

They would fly to the moon.

Big Dog did a lot of drawings.

Little Dog colored them in.

They made a list.

Big Dog took all the money from their
piggy bank. He gave it to Little Dog.
Little Dog went shopping and bought
the things they needed.

When Little Dog got back,

Big Dog checked the shopping.

There was cardboard, string,

tape, wallpaper paste,

rubber bands, plasticine,

and paint.

Big Dog cut out cardboard shapes.

Little Dog stuck them together

with tape.

Big Dog made important

rocket parts out of plasticine.

Little Dog tied them on with string.

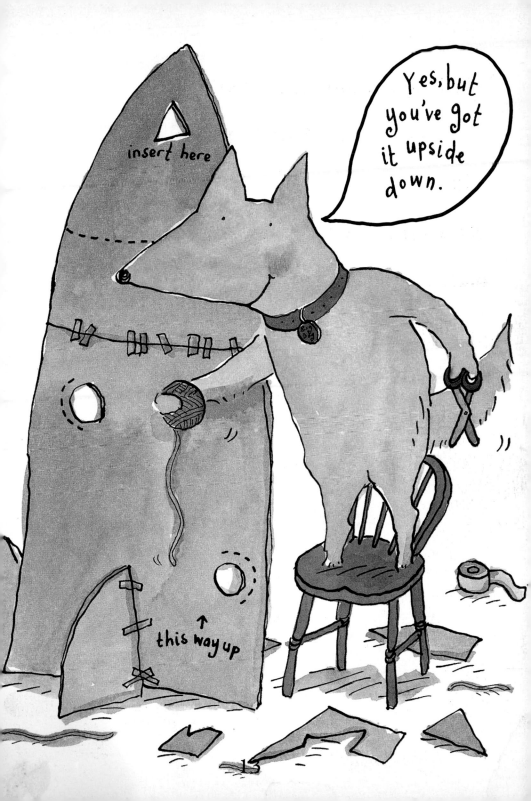

Little Dog ripped up some newspaper.

Big Dog mixed some wallpaper paste.

Then they stuck the newspaper all over

the cardboard and plasticine rocket.

They were tired after all their

cutting and sticking and pasting.

So they went to bed.

The moon shone outside the bedroom window. He glowed over the house in a gloomy way. He didn't know Big Dog and Little Dog were planning to visit him and cheer him up.

Wispy gray clouds hung around his eyes.

In the morning, Big Dog and Little Dog

woke early. They had a big breakfast.

Then they went to look at the rocket.

During the night the newspaper and paste had hardened. A big solid rocket stood on the carpet.

Little Dog went and got the paint.

Together they gave the rocket

two coats of shiny paint.

When it was dry, Big Dog

cut a door in the rocket.

19

Next, Big Dog cut out two windows.

Now they would each have

a window to look out of.

Big Dog grabbed his tool box.

He made an engine for the rocket.

(Just like that!)

21

Little Dog made sandwiches
while Big Dog washed his paws.
Then they filled a basket
with useful things
for the trip.

Now all they had to do was wait until the sun went to bed and the moon got up.

Big Dog and Little Dog watched.

At last, the moon woke up.

Little Dog and Big Dog sat in the rocket

and looked out of the windows.

They looked for the moon.

The rocket leaped into the sky.

It took them lumpity, bumpity

through the night.

It shot through the clouds.

It shot past the stars.

Lumpity, bumpity it took them

to the moon.

By the time Big Dog and Little Dog arrived,

the moon had gone to sleep again.

The rocket flew around him.

Moon just blinked his black eyes

and then went back to sleep.

So Big Dog gently landed

the rocket on Moon's head.

Moon opened his black eyes.

Big Dog and Little Dog hopped out and

walked down to Moon's ear to speak to him.

Moon began to smile a little smile.

The smile grew bigger and bigger . . .

. . . and bigger and bigger.

Soon it was a big cheesy grin.

Big Dog and Little Dog walked

all over the moon.

Hop, bop, jump, bump they went.

Moon's cheesy grin soon turned into a little laugh.

And a great big chuckle.

Moon was rolling around laughing. The wispy gray clouds under his eyes disappeared.

Moon couldn't stop laughing.

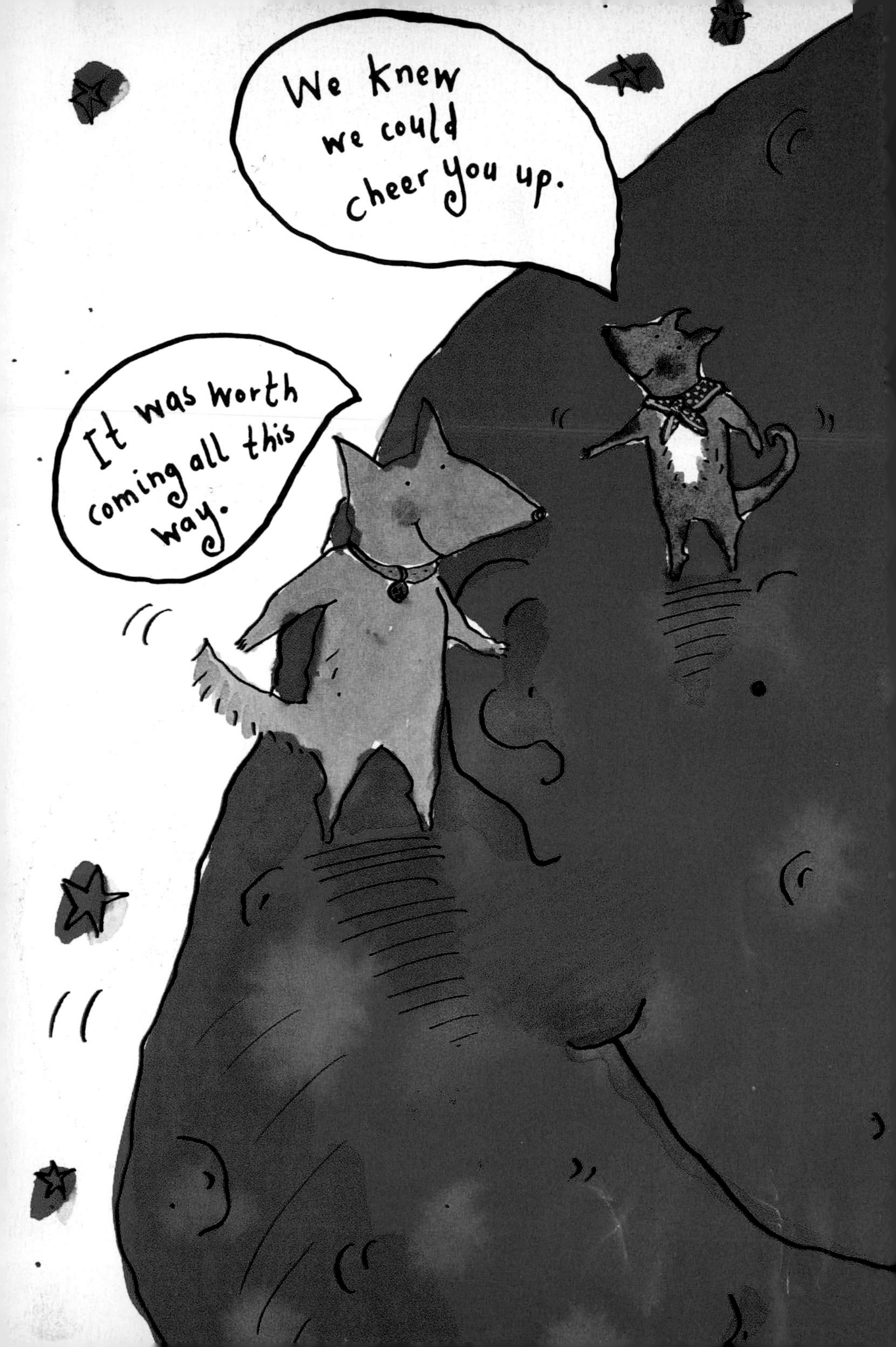
We knew we could cheer you up.
It was worth coming all this way.

So Big Dog and Little Dog

ran around the moon

while Moon grinned and giggled.

Soon Big Dog and Little Dog

were worn out

from so much running.

So Big Dog and Little Dog

went back to the rocket.

They ate their sandwiches

and rested their tired feet.

Big Dog and Little Dog flew home to bed.

Lumpity, bumpity through the night sky –

past the stars and through the clouds.

Gently, they landed

in their own

backyard.

Big Dog and Little Dog went straight to bed.

Soon they were fast asleep.

Moon shone down cheerfully on

Big Dog and Little Dog's house.

Big Dog and Little Dog

slept late the next morning.

When they woke up the moon had gone.

The sun was shining.

Big Dog cooked eggs

and toast for breakfast.

Now Big Dog and Little Dog

go and visit Moon every Monday.

Moon is happy every day now. . .

. . . but he likes Mondays best.